Dear Parents and Educators,

Welcome to Penguin Young Readers! As parents and educators, you know that each child develops at his or her own pace—in terms of speech, critical thinking, and, of course, reading. Penguin Young Readers recognizes this fact. As a result, each Penguin Young Readers book is assigned a traditional easy-to-read level (1–4) as well as a Guided Reading Level (A–P). Both of these systems will help you choose the right book for your child. Please refer to the back of each book for specific leveling information. Penguin Young Readers features esteemed authors and illustrators, stories about favorite characters, fascinating nonfiction, and more!

Corduroy's Garden

LEVEL 3

GUIDED READING LEVEL **J**

This book is perfect for a **Transitional Reader** who:
- can read multisyllable and compound words;
- can read words with prefixes and suffixes;
- is able to identify story elements (beginning, middle, end, plot, setting, characters, problem, solution); and
- can understand different points of view.

Here are some **activities** you can do during and after reading this book:
- Summarize: Work with the child to write a short summary about what happened in the story. What happened in the beginning? What happened in the middle? What happened at the end?.
- Adding -ing to Words: One of the rules when adding -ing to words is, when a word ends with an -e, take off the -e and add -ing. With other words, you simply add the -ing ending to the root word. The following words are -ing words in this story. On a separate piece of paper, write down the root word for each word: *raking, digging, watching, getting.* Next, add -ing to the following words from the story: *put, want, find, make, form, shut, take.*

Remember, sharing the love of reading with a child is the best gift you can give!

—Sarah Fabiny, Editorial Director
  Penguin Young Readers program

*Penguin Young Readers are leveled by independent reviewers applying the standards developed by Irene Fountas and Gay Su Pinnell in *Matching Books to Readers: Using Leveled Books in Guided Reading*, Heinemann, 1999.

PENGUIN YOUNG READERS
An Imprint of Penguin Random House LLC

Penguin supports copyright. Copyright fuels creativity, encourages diverse voices,
promotes free speech, and creates a vibrant culture. Thank you for buying an authorized edition
of this book and for complying with copyright laws by not reproducing, scanning, or distributing any
part of it in any form without permission. You are supporting writers and allowing Penguin to
continue to publish books for every reader.

Copyright © 2002 by Penguin Random House LLC. All rights reserved. First published in 2002 by
Viking Children's Books. This edition published in 2019 by Penguin Young Readers, an imprint of
Penguin Random House LLC, 345 Hudson Street, New York, New York 10014. Manufactured in China.

The Library of Congress has catalogued the Viking edition
under the following Control Number: 2001007635

ISBN 9781524790844 (pbk)   10 9 8 7 6 5 4 3 2 1
ISBN 9781524790851 (hc)   10 9 8 7 6 5 4 3 2 1

CORDUROY'S Garden

by Alison Inches
illustrated by Allan Eitzen
based on the characters created by Don Freeman

Penguin Young Readers
An Imprint of Penguin Random House

Dig! Dig! Dig!

Plop! Plop! Plop!

Pat! Pat! Pat!

"There!" said Lisa.

"My beans are all planted."

Lisa watered the seeds.

Then she picked up Corduroy.

"Come on, Corduroy," she said.

"I have an important job for you."

She took Corduroy inside and
put him in a chair by the window.
"I want you to watch the beans,"
said Lisa.
Then off she went to school.
"Wow," said Corduroy.
"I get to watch the beans!"

Corduroy got right to work.

He watched and watched.

He saw a man next door raking

and a lady walking her baby.

Soon, the sun began to

feel warm.

Corduroy yawned.

Ha hum!

Then Corduroy fell sound

asleep.

Jingle! Jingle! Jingle!

A puppy pushed open the gate

and began digging.

Dirt hit the window.

Corduroy woke up

and looked out.

"Oh no!" cried Corduroy.

"The beans!"

Rap! Rap! Rap!

Corduroy rapped on the window.

But the puppy kept digging.

And digging.

Then *plunk!*

The puppy put his bone

in the hole.

Flick! Flick! Flick!

He buried it

and left the garden.

"I have to find more seeds!"

said Corduroy.

Corduroy looked in Lisa's desk.

He looked under the bed.

"Why, here are some seeds!"

said Corduroy.

Corduroy put three seeds in his
pocket and went to the garden.

Dig! Dig! Dig!

Plop! Plop! Plop!

Pat! Pat! Pat!

"There!" said Corduroy.
"The beans are
all planted again."

"This time," said Corduroy,

"I will make sure

to watch the beans."

And he did.

He watched them on sunny days.

He watched them on rainy days.

He watched them on all the days

in between.

Soon three little shoots came up.

They grew and grew.

The stems wrapped around

the stakes.

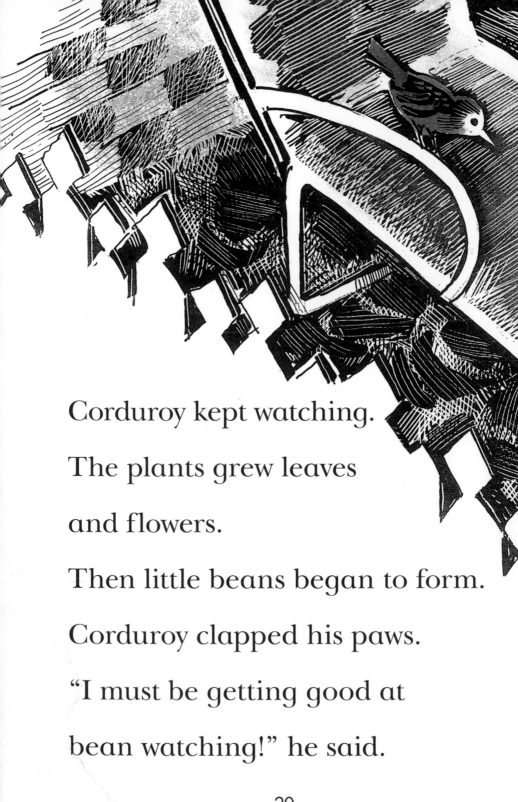

Corduroy kept watching.

The plants grew leaves

and flowers.

Then little beans began to form.

Corduroy clapped his paws.

"I must be getting good at

bean watching!" he said.

He put on his sunglasses

and got back to work.

Then *Jingle! Jingle! Jingle!*

Oh no! thought Corduroy.

The PUPPY!

The puppy was back for his bone.

The puppy stopped
and looked at Corduroy.

His ears went up.

"Arf!" said the puppy.

Corduroy shut his eyes.

But the puppy did not

take the bone.

He took Corduroy instead!

The puppy played toss

with Corduroy.

Corduroy flew up and down,

up and down!

Then the man next door said,

"NO!"

Thunk!

Corduroy fell to the ground.

The man picked Corduroy up
and dusted him off.
"I know where you live,"
said the man.
He took Corduroy home.
And just in time.

The school bus stopped out front.

Lisa ran through the garden gate.

"Oh, look!" she cried.

"I see beans on the vine!"

She picked up Corduroy

and ran to see.

Lisa held a bean in her hand.

She turned it from side to side.

"Oooh," said Lisa.

"This is *not* a bean!"

It's not? thought Corduroy.

Then what is it?

"It's a green pepper!" said Lisa.

A green pepper, thought Corduroy.

Is that good?

"I *love* green peppers!" said Lisa.

Oh, phew! thought Corduroy.

"Corduroy, you did a great job."

I always wanted to do a great job,

thought Corduroy.